The Last Rhino

Deborah Stevenson

Illustrated by Morgan Spicer

Published by

FROG PRINCE BOOKS

Edited by Krista Hill, L Talbott Editorial

Book Design by Jeanne Balsam Graphics

Other books by the award-winning team of
Deborah Stevenson & Morgan Spicer

Soaring Soren
Oy! Elephants!

Paperback ISBN: 978-1-7325410-4-7
eBook ISBN: 978-1-7325410-0-9
Library of Congress Control Number: 2018907851

First Edition, 2018

To Scott and Patrick ~

*with fondest memories of
the many hours we spent
together, reading and learning
about animals.*

Table of Contents

PART I: MAKING A PROMISE

Chapter 1   The Watering Hole   9
Chapter 2   Horns   13
Chapter 3   Poachers   17
Chapter 4   The Promise   23

PART II: KEEPING A PROMISE

Chapter 5   Raziya   29
Chapter 6   Lost   35
Chapter 7   Figs   39
Chapter 8   Jib and Jab   43
Chapter 9   Lights in the Dark   49
Chapter 10   Lions!   51
Chapter 11   Making a Stand   55
Chapter 12   The Plan   59
Chapter 13   The Celebration   62
Chapter 14   The Brightest Star   67
              Epilogue   71

LEARN MORE

The Names in This Story   74
About Rhinos   75
Rhino Fun Facts   78
About Rhinos and Birds   79
How Can You Help?   80
Acknowledgments   83

PART I: MAKING A PROMISE

The Watering Hole

Ayubu squinted up toward the cloudless African sky.

"Oh, no!" the baby rhino said. He blinked a few times from the sun's glare before he turned to his mother, Nthanda. "The sun is so hot, it's burning a hole in the sky!"

"It looks that way, Ayubu" his mother replied, "but I promise the sky will be fine."

Ayubu was relieved.

"On the other hand, *we* might just melt into rhino puddles in this heat," Nthanda added playfully. "We'd best cool off before it gets any hotter."

Mother and baby headed for the watering hole. They paused to watch as a graceful cattle egret circled above them. The white bird drifted down in big spirals, landing gently on Nthanda's back.

His name was Imari. He had been with Nthanda since long before Ayubu was born. Imari kept the mother rhino free of ticks and insects. This was not a great sacrifice. It just so happened these were his favorite foods. He also alerted the rhinos to dangers on the savanna.

"The coast looks clear," Imari said.

"Come, Ayubu," Nthanda said. "Let's get wet and have a drink."

The watering hole was peaceful. Zebras and antelopes waded in the shallow pool. A giraffe leaned down for a sip of water. Ayubu wondered how the water made it all the way up that long neck.

Ayubu and his mother paused at the water's edge. He spotted a young elephant across the way. She wasn't much bigger than he.

She filled her trunk with water and sprayed it at Ayubu. The cool spray felt good. Ayubu laughed and the little elephant smiled. Then she turned to follow her mother back to their herd.

Horns

Ayubu and his mother were cooler and no longer thirsty. After rolling in the mud to protect themselves from the sun and the insects, they headed toward the plain. Imari hitched a ride aboard Nthanda's shoulders. The rhinos would spend the afternoon grazing.

Ayubu turned to Imari. "Why are you always on the lookout?"

"I'm checking for danger," Imari replied.

"Lions?" Ayubu asked.

Imari nodded. "For one thing, yes—and poachers."

"Nothing is more dangerous to rhinos than poachers," Nthanda added.

Ayubu frowned. "What are poachers?"

"Poachers are people who break the laws of humans," Nthanda explained. "They hunt and kill rhinos."

"Once, there were many rhinos on these plains," Imari said. "Now, thanks to poachers, it's just you and your mother."

"Why do they want to kill us?" Ayubu asked.

Imari sighed. "Money."

"Yes," Nthanda agreed. "They want our horns to sell."

"Why?"

"Some people," said his mother, "believe rhino horns can cure diseases. Others simply think possessing something so rare makes them seem important."

Ayubu crossed his eyes to see if he had a horn. He did not—just a bump where one might be, someday. His mother and Imari laughed.

"You don't have horns yet, Ayubu dear.

You are too young." Nthanda's smile faded and she looked away. "Soon enough," she added quietly.

Ayubu sensed his mother's worry and felt uneasy. "Are all people poachers?" he asked.

"No," Nthanda replied. "Most people are good. Some even try to protect us."

Ayubu thought about that a moment. "I wish *all* people were good," he said.

His mother nuzzled him. "So do I, Ayubu."

Poachers!

Nthanda and Imari dozed in the late-afternoon shade. Ayubu watched as springboks played in the grass. They looked like miniature antelopes—tiny and quick. Two brothers chased each other. They paused to face off before butting heads, leaping in the air, and galloping off again. Ayubu envied them a little. He had no siblings to play with or chase.

Ayubu wandered off by himself.

"Stay where I can see you," Nthanda called after him.

"I will, Mother" he replied.

He went in search of logs and rocks. He rolled them over to see what crawly things lurked underneath. This kept him busy for a while, but when dusk came, it grew difficult to see. Ayubu started back toward his mother and Imari. As he walked, he thought again about the springbok brothers—and about his sister, Mbali.

When it was almost time for bed, Ayubu looked at his mother. "Tell me again about my father and Mbali."

The baby rhino had never known his father or his sister. Poachers had killed them before he was born. Ayubu loved to hear stories about them and begged his mother to tell them again and again.

"Your father was the bravest rhino in all of Africa," Nthanda said. "He wasn't afraid of anything!"

"Not even lions?" Ayubu's eyes grew wide.

Nthanda shook her head. "Not even lions. You are so much like him, Ayubu."

Ayubu liked that thought. He stood a

little taller with pride.

"Chasing butterflies was Mbali's favorite thing," Imari recalled. "Just imagine! A big rhino chasing a tiny butterfly—it was quite a sight!"

Ayubu saw his mother look at the sky and smile. He knew she was picturing Mbali chasing a butterfly.

Suddenly, hooves thundered as springboks fled the clearing. Imari quickly took flight to see what had startled them. In the distance, a Jeep barreled across the plain.

"Poachers!" Imari screeched. "Headed this way!"

Nthanda nudged Ayubu. "Run fast and stay with me!"

They were easy targets for poachers out in the open. The brush would be safer.

Ayubu struggled to keep up. His mother urged him onward as the Jeep gained on them. They tried to avoid the path of the bright headlights. The poachers were calling out.

They ducked into the cover of the brush. It was darker there, without the light from the moon. Ayubu did not see the vines until his feet got tangled in them. He fell hard. Nthanda quickly pushed him back to his feet and they took off again. The Jeep could not follow them in the dense brush. But they were not out of danger—the poachers could still follow on foot.

"Keep running!" Imari called out from above.

Once they had gotten a good lead on the poachers, they stopped to rest.

"That was close," Nthanda huffed.

"Too close," puffed Imari.

Surely the poachers could not be following them still. But they did not dare return to the clearing.

"We'll sleep here," said Nthanda.

Still shaken from the close call, Ayubu snuggled close to her.

"Sleep tight, my little Ayubu," Nthanda soothed.

She whispered, "I love you," but Ayubu

was too sleepy to answer. Instead, he nuzzled closer. Comforted by his mother's soft breathing and the quiet, steady sound of her heartbeat, the baby rhino drifted off to sleep.

When Ayubu awoke, the sun filtered through the trees in hazy bands of light. *Was last night just a bad dream?* He looked at the cuts on his legs from being tangled in the vines. It had not been a dream. Ayubu shook his head as he tried to wake up.

"I'm hungry!" he announced.

"What else is new?" his mother teased.

Imari laughed. "He *is* a growing rhino."

"That he is!" Nthanda agreed as she led them in the direction of the plain. "We'd better find you some breakfast before you starve. What would you like to—"

Suddenly, the earth beneath Nthanda's feet gave way.

The Promise

His mother had landed hard at the bottom of a deep pit trap set by poachers. Ayubu peered down into the pit, helpless, as she struggled to stand, but could not. His heart sank.

"Nthanda!" Imari squawked, swooping down next to her in the pit. "What is it?"

Nthanda winced.

"My shoulder."

She leaned in and whispered something to Imari.

"Always," Imari replied.

Ayubu watched his mother gaze at Imari for a moment before she looked up at him.

"Go with Imari, Ayubu!" Nthanda ordered. "Run as fast and as far as you can!"

"No! I won't go without you!" Ayubu protested. "You can't make me!"

"You *must*, Ayubu," his mother said.

"*No!* I ... can't! I ... *won't!*" Ayubu was sobbing now.

Imari flew up out of the pit, landed on Ayubu's head and nuzzled him reassuringly.

"Ayubu, listen to me," his mother said calmly. "You will be the last rhino now. I know it's hard, but I need you to be very brave. Promise me you will be brave and survive."

"I promise," Ayubu replied through his tears.

His mother had tears in her eyes, too. She spoke softly, and Ayubu clung to each word as if it were a gentle embrace: "When you look up at the night sky, search for the brightest star. That will be me, telling you good night and how much I love you. Now you *must* run."

Ayubu was sure the pang he felt in his chest was his heart breaking, but he did as he was told. He could not bear to look back, so he simply ran. He crashed through the brush, with Imari showing the way from above. All the anger and hurt he felt, he put into running, as hard and as fast as he could.

Once they were safely away, Imari called out, "We can stop now, Ayubu."

Ayubu kept running. Imari touched down in front of him.

"Stop, Ayubu!" cried the cattle egret.

Ayubu stopped, breathing hard. He closed his eyes tightly and lowered his head. A tear rolled down his nose. "I won't see her again, will I?" he asked.

Imari let out a long sigh. "No," he replied.

PART II: KEEPING A PROMISE

Raziya

Months passed. Each afternoon, Ayubu and Imari walked to the watering hole. Ayubu grazed on the plains while Imari kept watch. Each night, they slept in the little clearing that was home. Ayubu grew bigger and his horns started to grow, too.

"You are not a baby anymore, Ayubu," Imari told him one day, as they headed to the watering hole.

Imari perched on Ayubu's nose and inspected his horn. "You have grown into a handsome, young rhino."

"Thanks, Imari," Ayubu said.

"Most welcome," answered the bird.

"No, I mean for everything," said Ayubu. "I don't know what I would do without you."

"I can never replace your mother," said Imari, hopping down to the ground. "But I am always here for you."

Ayubu nuzzled Imari. The bird was a devoted friend and a loyal guardian. Still, he missed his mother. It was difficult and, at times, scary without her. But he tried to honor his promise to Nthanda to be brave, like his father.

When they arrived at the watering hole, Ayubu spotted a young elephant. She had grown too, but even so, he recognized her. She was the little elephant who had splashed him that day long ago.

"I'm Raziya," she said. "You look like you could use some company. Would you like to walk with me for a bit?"

Her kindness touched Ayubu. He followed her and they strolled together around the watering hole. They chatted

about the other animals. A giraffe spread his long legs and bent his long neck down to drink.

"Do you know how the giraffe gets water all the way up that long neck?" Ayubu asked.

Raziya laughed. "Not a clue," she said. Ayubu laughed too.

"Want to swim?" Raziya asked.

"Sure!" Ayubu replied.

The cool water was refreshing. Ayubu spied a shiny stone at the bottom of the watering hole. Raziya reached down and picked it up with her trunk. She held it out so Ayubu could inspect it. The stone was a dull gray and had beautiful flecks of gold that sparkled in the sunlight.

"It seems plain at first," Ayubu said, squinting to see it better, "but when you look closely, it's kind of unique and special!"

"Just like us!" Raziya said. She laughed and tossed the stone back into the water, splashing Ayubu in the process. He splashed her back. A fierce battle began, and continued until they were both exhausted. They rested and had just started playing a quiet game of "I Spy," when Imari said it was time to go.

After that, Ayubu and Imari often spent afternoons with Raziya's herd. While Ayubu and Raziya played, Imari enjoyed the chance to visit with the other birds.

Lost

One afternoon, Ayubu and Raziya were running sprints to see who was faster. The sun beat down on the plains and the heat weighed on them like a heavy blanket.

"Let's find some shade," Raziya suggested.

"I'd better tell Imari where we're going," Ayubu said.

He glanced over at Imari. The bird was dozing on a rock.

"He's asleep," said Raziya. "He'll never even notice you're gone."

"I guess you're right," Ayubu said. "We

won't be long." He followed Raziya.

The two wandered away from the elephant herd and headed for the brush.

"Don't go too far," Raziya's mother called after them.

"Okay," Raziya huffed. "We're just heading over to the shade to cool off."

Ayubu could tell Raziya was annoyed. "She just worries about you," he said.

"She worries too much," Raziya complained.

Ayubu understood. Still, he could not help wishing Nthanda were there to worry about *him*.

Raziya seemed to read his mind. "Do you miss her terribly?" she asked.

"Yes," Ayubu admitted. "It seems like everyone but me has a family."

Raziya rested her trunk gently on his shoulders as they walked.

After a while, he asked, "Do you ever wish you had a brother or sister?"

"I do have a brother," Raziya replied. "You, Ayubu. You are my little brother."

Ayubu swallowed hard. He felt the

same way about Raziya, but he could not find the words to tell her. So, he bumped Raziya gently with his shoulder instead. She bumped him back.

"Race you!" Ayubu challenged.

They laughed and started to run.

The two were having a wonderful game. They raced around tree after tree, trying to see how tightly they could turn around them. They leaned in, so that they almost touched the tree trunks. Over and over, Ayubu and Raziya raced around the trees, trying to turn tighter and run faster.

Breathless from running and laughing, they dropped down beside a pile of boulders to rest.

"You're pretty fast—*for a girl!*" Ayubu teased.

"You're pretty fast—*for a rhino!*" Raziya teased back.

It had grown darker while they were playing.

"It must be getting late," Ayubu said. "Maybe we'd better head back to the herd."

"I guess so," Raziya agreed. "Which way is the plain?"

Ayubu thought for a moment before he nodded in one direction. "This way," he said, trying to sound sure. But he was not sure.

The two set out. They tried to backtrack the way they had come.

"We have to be almost there," said Ayubu. "We've been walking *forever*."

"Oh, no!" Raziya groaned.

"What?" Ayubu's eyes followed to where Raziya's trunk was pointing. Then he saw it — the pile of boulders where they had stopped to rest earlier.

"We've gone in a circle!" Raziya said.

Figs

They had gone to the right before, so this time they tried going left.

"Does this baobab tree look familiar?" Ayubu asked hopefully, nodding his head toward the funny looking tree. He was always amused by baobab trees. It was as if the tops were underground and the roots were sticking up into the sky. They looked like someone had turned them upside down.

"I think so," said Raziya, "but I'm not sure."

They continued onward. Ayubu was not

at all certain they were headed the right way.

"Did you hear something?" Raziya asked.

Ayubu frowned. "Like what?"

"Rustling ... from above us."

Ayubu shrugged. They looked up at the rock fig trees, but saw nothing. They took a few more steps before Ayubu suddenly stopped.

"I heard it that time!" he said.

"Walk faster," Raziya whispered.

As Ayubu and Raziya quickened their pace, the rustling got faster too. They stopped ... the rustling stopped. Something was following them!

"*OUCH!*" Ayubu cried as a fig hit him in the eye.

"*HEY!*" Raziya shouted as two more figs bounced off her back.

They heard giggling coming from above. Then, lots of figs rained down on them. A frenzy of giggling followed.

"Come out and show yourselves!" Ayubu demanded.

"Come out and show yourselves!" a tiny voice mocked. This was followed by more giggles.

Raziya tried a different approach. "Please do come out," she said sweetly. "We'd love to thank you properly for these wonderful figs!"

Jib and Jab

Plop! Plop! First one little Vervet monkey and then a second dropped from the tree and stood in front of them.

"Jib, at your service!" said the first monkey.

"Jab. Pleased to meet you!" said the second.

"Pleased to meet you, too," replied Rayiza.

Ayubu just grunted. He was still annoyed about the figs—and the mocking.

"We're a little lost," Raziya said. "Could you tell us which way to the plain?"

"This way!" Jib said, pointing in one direction.

"That way!" Jab said, pointing in another.

"Umm, how can it be this way and that way at the same time?" Raziya asked.

Jib had a white band across his forehead. Beneath it, his mischievous eyes shone brightly from his otherwise black face. When he wrinkled his forehead, the resulting expression was comical and perplexed at the same time. Jab scratched his head and rubbed his whiskers. The pair thought a minute.

"That way!" Jib said. He pointed right.

"This way!" Jab countered, and pointed left.

Ayubu rolled his eyes. "This is hopeless," he said.

"You can climb to the top of this tree, can't you?" Raziya asked the monkeys.

Jib and Jab giggled.

"Of course we can!" Jib said.

"We're *monkeys*!" Jab added.

"Sorry. Silly question," Raziya said.

"What I meant to say was, '*would* you climb this tree?'"

"Why would we?" asked Jab.

"Why indeed?" added Jib.

"If you did, you could see the plain," said Raziya. "And you could tell us which way it is from here."

"I'm sure we *could*," said Jib.

"But I'm not at all sure we *would*," said Jab.

"Oh, for goodness sake!" Ayubu blurted. "What would it take for you to climb the tree?"

"*Weeeell*," said Jib, eyeing a large log in front of Ayubu. "There is that matter of the big log."

"Indeed," said Jab. "We would *loooove* it if someone would roll over that big log."

"Too heavy for us," Jib chattered.

"Much too heavy," Jab echoed.

"We just know the best, tastiest bugs are under that log," Jib added.

"Done!" said Ayubu, lowering his head and shoving the log until it rolled over.

Jib and Jab made a beeline for the log, but Ayubu quickly stepped in and blocked their path. Jib stopped short and Jab ran into him from behind. Raziya tried not to laugh.

Ayubu took another step toward the monkeys. "Before you eat a single bug, you will climb that tree."

Jab raised one white eyebrow. Jib raised the opposite eyebrow. A beetle scurried across the log and Jab's stomach growled—rather loudly.

"Well, off we go then," said Jab.

"After you," said Jib.

The pair scurried up the tree to the very top. They looked out.

"Plain!" they said at once, both pointing to the left.

Raziya waved her trunk at the monkeys in appreciation. "Thank you!" she shouted.

Ayubu just grunted, turned and followed her toward the plain. He heard more giggling as one last fig whizzed past his ear.

Lights in the Dark

Now that Ayubu and Raziya were headed in the right direction, it did not take them long to reach the plain. As they stepped out of the brush, they could see the sun setting ahead of them.

"Now we can just follow the sun home," Ayubu said hopefully.

"Well, we had better hurry," Raziya replied. "It doesn't look like the sun plans to wait too long for us."

His friend was right. The sun was setting quickly now. Their shadows grew longer, then slowly disappeared as darkness spread over the plain. If not for the glow from the moon, they could not have seen their own feet as they walked.

"Maybe we should call for help," Ayubu suggested. "The herd can't be too far away."

Raziya rolled her eyes. "You know how my mother worries. If I admit I got lost, she'll attach me to her trunk and never let me out of her sight again."

"Probably so," Ayubu agreed. He thought of Imari. The bird would not be pleased that he had gone off without telling him. "But they must be looking for us by now."

"We can just keep walking in this direction," said Raziya. "It will be fine."

"It will be fine," Ayubu repeated. But he was feeling uneasy. He looked straight ahead, then to the side, and then behind them. They were surrounded by glowing pairs of yellow-green lights. EYES!

"Raziya!" Ayubu said in an urgent whisper. "I don't think we're alone anymore."

Lions!

Ayubu directed Raziya's gaze with his head.

"Lions!" Raziya whispered, her eyes wide with fear.

"*Lots* of them," Ayubu replied.

"Any ideas?" Raziya asked.

Before Ayubu could answer, they heard a long, low growl. A lioness burst from the grass to their right. A second approached from the other side.

"They want to separate us!" Raziya cried. "Whatever you do, don't let them!"

Raziya and Ayubu stood back to back.

Ayubu charged at the lioness coming towards him. Another lioness grabbed onto him from behind. Her strong claws stung as they dug into his thick skin. Raziya whirled around and slapped the lioness away with her trunk, sending her tumbling.

A third lioness grabbed Raziya. Ayubu bit down hard on the attacker's ear. The lioness howled and ran away.

Despite their small victories, they could not hold the lions off for long. Raziya raised her trunk and trumpeted as loudly as she could, again and again. Ayubu guarded her as she called for help. Whenever a big cat approached, he lowered his head and charged—but for each lioness he fended off, it seemed there were two more.

The ground began to tremble beneath them.

"Keep calling!" Ayubu urged. "The herd is coming!"

Raziya's trumpets were drowned out in the thunder of elephants as the herd descended on the lions.

It was difficult to tell what happened next, it all went so quickly. A lioness went sailing through the air while other lions scrambled in all directions. The big cats were no match for a herd of angry elephants. As suddenly as they had appeared, the lions were gone.

Imari landed on Ayubu's shoulders. He was breathing hard. "Thank goodness we found you! I was so worried!"

"I'm sorry," Ayubu said. He meant it.

"Are you two okay?" Raziya's mother asked.

She embraced Raziya protectively with her trunk. Raziya hugged her back.

"Fine," said Ayubu.

"Just a few scratches," Raziya added.

"I can't believe you ..." Raziya's mother started to say, and then stopped. She took a deep breath. "Everyone is safe now. That's the important thing. Let's go home and get some sleep."

Ayubu and Raziya bumped shoulders gently as they followed the herd in silence.

Making A Stand

Raziya's mother did not have to warn them again about wandering off. After their adventure with the lions, Raziya and Ayubu were careful. They did not venture out on their own unless an adult from the herd or Imari was with them.

One day, they were looking for tasty shrubs. They talked and laughed while Imari acted as lookout. Ayubu saw a brightly colored butterfly and decided to chase it.

"Look!" he called out happily to Imari. "I'm Mbali, chasing a butterfly!"

Raziya joined him. Imari eyed the butterfly with a hungry look.

"Hey! No eating our butterfly for lunch!" Ayubu scolded, trying to sound stern. Then he laughed.

Imari shrugged. He joined in the game instead.

They were having so much fun. They did not realize how far they had wandered. And they did not see the telltale straw until it was too late.

"*Aaahh!*" Raziya cried as she tumbled into the poacher's pit.

"*Noooo!*" Ayubu wailed.

"Don't panic!" Imari squawked from above, flapping his wings wildly.

Imari looked like he was already panicking.

"Are you hurt?" Ayubu asked.

"I'm fine," Raziya replied, "if you don't count the fact that I'm at the bottom of a poacher's pit."

Raziya was trying to sound tough. But Ayubu could hear the fear in his friend's voice. She was fighting back tears. He tried to reassure her. "You're little and not as heavy as a grown elephant. There has to be a way to get you out."

This could NOT be happening again! Not to Raziya! He thought hard, desperate for an idea.

Ayubu stomped his foot. "No, no, NO!" he cried out.

Frustrated and angry, he rammed his head into a nearby tree. A vine, loosened by the jolt, fell on him. He looked up at the trees and his eyes narrowed.

"I have a plan!" Ayubu announced. He turned to Imari, who was pacing on a nearby branch. "Fly and get the other birds! Tell them to bring their elephants."

"I can't just leave you here," Imari protested. "Your mother would want me to keep you safe."

"I'm *not* leaving this time!" Ayubu insisted. "My mother would want me to be brave!"

Not much can match the stubbornness of a determined rhino. Ayubu would not budge, and in the end, Imari had no choice but to give in.

The Plan

Imari flew off in the direction of the savanna where the elephants grazed. Ayubu and Raziya tried to pass the time. They did not want to think about the danger they were in.

"Let's play 'I Spy,'" Ayubu suggested.

"Okay," said Raziya. "You first."

Ayubu looked about. "I spy with my little eye, an antelope," he said.

"I spy with my little eye, a rock," Raziya answered.

"I spy with my little eye, a zebra," Ayubu replied.

"I spy with my little eye, a tree root," Raziya said, sounding impatient. "There's really not much to spy down here in this pit, Ayubu."

"I know," Ayubu said. *Please hurry, Imari,* he thought to himself.

It wasn't long, but it seemed like forever until Ayubu heard the thunder of stampeding elephants. Above the trees he spotted Imari, leading a formation of birds. There were white cattle egrets and smaller, gray oxpeckers. Below them was an army of elephants.

The elephants were eager to help. At Ayubu's direction, they reached up into the trees and pulled down vine after vine.

The egrets and oxpeckers collected the vines. The birds swooped into the pit, carefully looping each vine under Raziya's belly.

This continued until all the vines were in place. Then, the elephants formed a circle around the hole in the ground. They gathered up the vines in their trunks and began to pull, backing away from the pit.

Little by little, the vines tightened beneath Raziya. They lifted her off the ground, higher and higher, until finally she was able to scramble out of the pit.

The Celebration

The birds cheered. The elephants lifted Ayubu and Raziya in the air in celebration. When they were safely deposited back on the ground, Raziya's mother pushed through the jubilant herd.

"I don't know how to thank you, Ayubu," Raziya's mother said, hugging the young rhino.

"You're my hero!" Raziya whispered to Ayubu.

Ayubu blushed. Raziya bumped his shoulder.

"Why don't you and Imari stay with us

tonight," Raziya's mother offered.

"Thank you," said Ayubu. "But maybe another time."

Ayubu was not in the mood for company. Now that the danger was behind them, emotion had caught up with him.

The friends promised to meet up the next day at the watering hole. Ayubu watched as the elephants headed off across the plain. Raziya's mother pulled her daughter close; Raziya glanced back at Ayubu and rolled her eyes. Ayubu gave her a wink and chuckled to himself. He knew Raziya was relieved to be safe in her mother's embrace.

After they had gone, Imari said, "Your plan was ingenious, Ayubu."

"Thank you for trusting me," Ayubu replied. "You're a true friend, Imari. You've always been there for my family. Now you *are* my family."

Imari nuzzled the wide place between Ayubu's eyes. "I've always got your back," he joked. With that, he fluttered onto Ayubu's back, snatching a fly that had landed there.

Ayubu laughed.

"Let's go look for your dinner," Imari said, smacking his beak as he swallowed the fly. "And I'll have mine on the way."

He searched Ayubu's thick, rough skin for more tasty morsels, while Ayubu munched on grass. They walked in comfortable silence, enjoying the beautiful show as the bright orange sun slipped lazily behind the savanna.

The Brightest Star

Ayubu stared up at the night sky. A tear slowly made its way down his cheek.

"I miss her too," Imari said softly. "She would have been so proud of you today, Ayubu."

Ayubu swallowed hard. He looked up at the stars for a long time, searching. Just as his mother had promised, a bright star appeared. It seemed to wink at him. Ayubu felt his mother's presence. The feeling was, oddly, both comforting and sad.

Soon, Ayubu heard Imari's soft snoring. He was lucky to have a friend like Imari.

And he was so relieved that Raziya was safe. He loved them both dearly.

Still, there was an empty place in Ayubu's heart. He lay on the cool ground, thinking: *I will never again look into the face of somebody else like me.* Ayubu gazed up at the star for a moment, took a deep breath and closed his eyes. "I am the last rhino," he said, quietly. "I will be brave and survive."

He opened his eyes again and blinked back a tear. In that instant, the bright star seemed to blink back. Then, it grew brighter still. Ayubu settled into the tall grass. He smiled up at the sky.

"Goodnight, Mother," he said, and he drifted off to sleep.

Epilogue

Far, far across the savanna, a young
rhino looked up at the night sky. A
cattle egret stood beside her.
The rhino locked her gaze on the
brightest star. Then she recited, "Star
light, star bright, first star I see tonight,
I wish I may, I wish I might,
have the wish I wish tonight."
She closed her eyes and wished
with all her might.
"What was your wish, dear?"
asked the cattle egret.
"Same as always," the sleepy rhino
yawned. "I wished for
somebody else like me."

Learn More

The Names in this Story

This story takes place in Africa. The characters have African names, chosen because of their meanings. They may be difficult to pronounce, since they are not familiar. This section explains how to pronounce each name and what each means.

Nthanda (n-TAHN-dah) Star
Ayubu (ah-YOO-boo) One who continues to fight, even when there are obstacles
Imari (i-MAHR-ee) Faithful, loyal
Raziya (rah-ZEE-ah) Good-natured, friendly
Mbali (m-BAH-lee) Flower
Baobab (BOW-bab or BAY-ah-bab) The baobab is a tree native to Africa. It has a very wide trunk.

About Rhinos

Thankfully, this story is fiction. That means it is made up. Hopefully there will never be a "last" rhino, but the earth's rhinoceros population is in danger. Rhinos need our help if they are to survive.

One risk to rhinos is the loss of their habitats (the places where rhinos live). Humans keep moving into areas where wildlife lives. The wildlife has less space in which to roam and feed. Poaching is an even greater risk to rhinos. Poachers hunt, capture and kill rhinos for their horns. Some cultures believe rhino horns cure illnesses. This has never been proven to be true.

Poaching is against the law, but that does not stop it from happening. Criminal networks around the world are at the heart of the poaching problem. They sell illegally obtained rhino horns in countries far, far away from Africa. The criminals make a lot of money doing this. They have no regard for the suffering they cause the animals, and no concern about robbing the planet of these magnificent creatures. Many poachers are simply poor, local people, desperate to earn a living for themselves and their families. Like the endangered animals they are paid to hunt, the poachers are also being exploited by these criminal networks.

When a kind of animal no longer exists, it is said to be "extinct." For example, dinosaurs are extinct. They once lived on the planet, but now they do not. There are groups of people who work to protect rhinos so they won't become extinct. They raise money to fight poaching and the criminals that promote it. They guard and protect rhinos and their habitats. They study rhinos and educate the public about them. They set up places where rhinos can live safely and breed. And they support programs that help the African economy so that people have other ways to earn a living besides poaching. This helps make sure there will be future generations of rhinos.

Rhino Fun Facts

◆ The word "rhinoceros" means "nose horn."

◆ Rhinos like to step in their own dung (that's a fancy word for poop). They do this so they can leave their scent behind when they walk. This lets others know they've been there.

◆ There are five species of rhinos in the world today: Black, White, Sumatran, Greater One-Horned and Javan.

◆ Black as well as white rhinos are actually grey in color.

◆ A rhino's horn is made of keratin. This is the same substance that makes up your hair and nails.

◆ Rhinos have poor eyesight, but excellent senses of smell and hearing.

◆ A large group of rhinos is called a "crash."

About Rhinos & Birds

Sometimes you hear someone say, "I'll scratch your back, and you scratch mine." (It's not easy to scratch your own back. Go ahead—try it.) This saying means "you help me do something that it is difficult for me to do myself and, in return, I'll help you do something that is difficult for you."

In nature, this kind of relationship is called symbiosis (sim-by-OH-sis). Rhinos and birds may seem unlikely friends, but they are symbiotic. Rhinos are bothered by insects, like flies and ticks. They don't have hands to swat away these pests themselves. Birds, like cattle egrets and oxpeckers, sit on the rhinos and feed on these insects. This helps the rhinos. In turn, the rhinos help the birds by providing a sort of four-legged restaurant. The birds also help rhinos by alerting them to danger.

How Can You Help?

LEAD the Charge:
Learn, Educate, Adopt, Donate!

One of the most important ways to help rhinos is to **LEARN** more about them. They are magnificent animals. By getting to know them better, we can understand why it is so important to make sure they survive.

EDUCATE others about what you learn. That way they will care about helping rhinos, too.

ADOPT a rhino who needs your help! A number of rhino conservation groups offer adoption programs to help orphaned baby rhinos.

For information on some of the programs available, visit *www.FrogPrinceBooks.net.* This is a fun way to get to know a rhino that needs your protection.

Start a project to raise money for rhino conservation efforts. **DONATE** to organizations who work to help protect rhinos and other endangered species. For ideas, visit *www.FrogPrinceBooks.net*!

Be A Rhino Hero!

Acknowledgments

Deepest thanks to the many dedicated people who work so tirelessly to ensure rhinos have a future in our world.

Thank you to Carol McCallum and International Rhino Foundation for their input on facts about rhinos and their habitat.

A huge thank you to my very talented partners, illustrator, Morgan Spicer, editor, Krista Hill and book designer, Jeanne Balsam, for their invaluable support and collaboration on this project. I could not have done it without you!

Tribal pattern graphic - interior and back cover:
Liza Ievleva/Shutterstock.com

About the Author & Illustrator

The Last Rhino reunites an award-winning team: author **Deborah Stevenson** and illustrator **Morgan Spicer.** Their picture books have won numerous awards, including Best Children's Non-Fiction Book, Next Generation Indie Book Awards for *Soaring Soren: When French Bulldogs Fly* and Feathered Quill's Best Children's Animal Book for *Oy, Elephants!*

Stevenson and Spicer share a passion for animals that is the heart and soul of their collaboration, and a strong desire to share that passion with children. *The Last Rhino* is their first chapter book. Deborah enjoyed the freedom to explore more complex plots and characters, and Morgan, the opportunity to utilize her formidable talents in black and white illustrations. For both, the driving force behind this project was to raise awareness and funds to help perilously endangered rhinos survive for future generations.

Deborah
Stevenson

Photo © M. Nicole Fisher Photography

In addition to sharing her love of animals with children, Deborah Stevenson's books convey positive messages about believing in your abilities–to achieve your goals, to make positive differences in the world, and to be kind to yourself and others. A former technical writer, literature major, and a mother, children's books have proven to be a perfect outlet for Deborah's interests. She lives in New Jersey with a few too many dogs, but wouldn't trade any of them. When she is not marketing telecomm products at her day job, or writing, she enjoys training for and competing in the sport of dog agility.

Morgan Spicer

Morgan Spicer, like Stevenson, believes kindness can make a world of difference in anyone's life, be it a young reader, a parent or a four-legged friend. Vegan and dog mom, Spicer will one day open the doors to a creative and cruelty-free oasis: a place where humans and animals, young and old, can come together every day, to celebrate the beauty of nature and embrace the importance of kindness and compassion. Morgan Spicer has illustrated over twenty children's books. She lives in the woods by the beach with her four rescue dogs and her husband.